I0788196

for

P&M

who aided and abetted my love affair with all things Cornish

Foreword

Some might say that to be truly Cornish, you must be born west of the Tamar, preferably to parents of similar good fortune, and ideally both sets of grandparents too. It's quite a tall order, and not everyone is lucky enough to meet such strict criteria. It can seem a little harsh, especially given that no one is given the choice in where we pop out. The term 'Cornish by design', therefore, goes some way to assuaging those of us who can never claim to be 'Cornish by birth'.

When Tanya Brittain approached me with the idea of writing a regular column for *Cornwall Today* magazine, she was already familiar to me as a musician and event organiser active on the Cornwall circuit. Her proposal – a monthly column documenting her attempts to learn Kernewek, the Cornish language, from scratch – was a happy coincidence, as such a position had been only recently vacated.

Our readers, both in Kernow and beyond, are passionate about Cornwall and its heritage, and Kernewek mines a rich seam of content. Who better to fill this gap than Tanya, who had won the International Pan-Celtic Song Contest with Hal-an-Tow, inspired by that most Cornish of festivals, Helston Flora Day?

She turned out to be the perfect fit. Engaging, witty and relatable, her style was the best introduction to one of Cornwall's most treasured attributes, her dedication to the cause evident in every carefully chosen word. Sometimes she would draw upon a local tradition or festival; at other times, personal anecdotes would come to the fore. I was relieved, upon receiving an interview with a Canadian Cousin Jenny, to know that it wouldn't be followed by travel expenses.

I thoroughly enjoyed reading Tanya's contributions each month, and you are fortunate in not having to wait for each instalment, but can indulge in one sitting if you wish, much like binge-watching the box-set of your choice on catch-up TV.

The only thing left to say is: **omlowenhe** (enjoy), and if inspired, find a class and take up Kernewek for yourself.

Kirstie Newton
Editor

Cornwall Today Magazine
cornwalltoday.co.uk

Cornish language – why bother?

Twelve years ago, my children came home from their first day at primary school repeating the words "**Myttin da, Miss Harvey**". It was only at this point that I realised Cornwall had its own language, and my children were expected to greet their teacher in Cornish each morning.

I'd always known Cornwall was different somehow, but could never quite put my finger on why. As a regular visitor to the Cornish coast with my scuba diving club, I knew about its beautiful landscape, rugged coastline, and marine life but it was only after living here for a few years that I really started to understand how many unique features Cornwall has, language being one of them.

I'm Breton by ancestry but I was born and raised in a small mining town in South Yorkshire. It was community of tough, highly opinionated working-class people; a place not unlike the small harbour town of Looe, where I ended up living forty years later. When I was growing up, accent and dialect varied hugely from one Yorkshire community to the next. Now of course, things are different; we no longer live and work in one place all our lives. We travel, we relocate, we commute. We meet and marry people from other places, our children are born in different counties and sometimes in different countries.

Having discovered that we'd moved to a place with its own language, I immediately felt an obligation to learn more. After all, if I'd moved to France instead of Cornwall, I would greet people with a cheery *"Bonjour, ça va?"* So, why not do the same in Cornwall?

I'm not fluent in French, but I did once manage to order breakfast in my hotel room whilst on holiday there. I successfully fielded the questions about tea or coffee, black or white, croissants or rolls – but panicked slightly when I was asked for my room number. It was room three hundred and nine, and after an embarrassingly long pause, I managed *trois – zero – neuf.* My breakfast arrived and my efforts where politely acknowledged. I felt good about myself. It didn't change the world, but at least I'd made the effort.

There are over two hundred and twenty million French speakers around the world, so there are plenty of opportunities to speak the language. When it comes to Cornish however, it's a different story. Although the number of speakers has grown rapidly in recent years, there are still only about five thousand people able to speak any Cornish at all, consequently practicing conversational Cornish can be a challenge.

So why bother?

Because it's part of what makes Cornwall different. Language is part of our heritage and cultural identity. Cornish is one of only six British and Irish minority languages protected by the European Charter for Regional Minority Languages, which covers seventy-nine different tongues. The others are Welsh, Scots (Ulster Scots in Northern Ireland), Scottish Gaelic, Irish and Manx Gaelic.

Some elements of Cornish culture seem to be better celebrated overseas than on home turf, but that's no surprise when you consider that between 1860 and 1900 two hundred and fifty thousand people (two thirds of the population) left Cornwall for the United States, Australia, South America and Canada. It's estimated there are six million people worldwide with Cornish ancestry, but fewer than ten percent of them live in Cornwall. The Cornish diaspora are still very engaged with their language, music and dance. Our roots are important, and now more than ever, we seem to have a need to belong.

Where are you from? How do you answer that question? Do you state your exact place of birth? The town you were brought up in? Is it where your parents are from? Or is it where your heart is and where you feel you *should* be?

It's an endless debate. In the meantime, I'm absorbing the culture of the place I now call home, and I'm doing my best to learn **Kernewek** (Cornish). Even if I just learn the basics like *'Hello, how are you?'* and *'See you later'*. It won't change the world, but at least I'll have made the effort.

Dydh da, fatla genes? | Hello, how are you?

Dha weles diwettha! | See you later!

Oy! How do you like your eggs?

Imagine my delight when I discovered that the Cornish word for egg is '**oy**'. Finally, a word I can pronounce and one I won't forget in a hurry. I can't stop saying it. Who would have thought the humble egg (**oy uvel**) could be so inspiring!

Synonymous with surprises, eggs are considered a symbol of fertility and new life, unless they're rotten and thrown of course, in which case they're an expression of disapproval. Meringues, pasty glazes, soufflés, omelettes, cakes, custard, and mayonnaise all rely on eggs for lift, shine and consistency. Highly decorated ones are coveted. Egg white can be found in cleaning products, beauty preparations, paint and traditional photographic processes. The multi-tasking egg can also make a handy sports day prop, a useful hangover cure and an effective slug repellent.

Personally, I like mine poached, with a pinch of Cornish sea salt and a splash of vinegar. Right now, however, I really want to order scrambled egg on toast.

Waitress: What can I get you for breakfast madam?
Me: **Oy skramblys war grasen, mar pleg**

What's not to like about the translation of scrambled egg on toast? Maybe a fried egg is more your thing though, in which case make sure you ask for **oy friys** with your full Cornish breakfast.

In the run up to Easter, millions of foil-wrapped chocolate eggs line the supermarket aisles. Whatever the origin of the Easter egg (**oy Pask**), a simple chocolate egg (**oy choklet**) clearly makes us happy (**lowen**).

In April, in Cornwall you can expect lots of **glaw** (rhymes with cow). '**Glaw, glaw ha moy glaw**' translates into English as 'Rain, rain and more rain'.

Sunshine and showers in equally proportions – isn't that one of the reasons why Cornwall is so lush? Wales seems to have its fair share of **glaw** too, in fact Cornish and Welsh language share the same word for rain.

Ah well, it'll soon be summer – at which point I'm hoping to be drier, warmer and more fluent in Cornish. In the meantime, my conversations will be short, painfully slow and fairly superficial but I'm starting to spot words I recognise in other people's conversations. I've started using basic Cornish greetings in my emails which is great way to raise awareness, plus it gives you time to consider what you want to say. The odd Cornish word here and there on social media also helps. I challenge myself to translate and use a new phrase every day, I don't get it right every time, but as the saying goes 'you can't make an omelette without breaking a few eggs'.

Oy da | Good egg

Yar hag oy | Chicken and egg

Oy choklet | Chocolate egg

Oy neyth | Nest egg

Oy Pask
Easter Egg

Oy owrek
Golden egg

Oy war dha vejeth
Egg on your face

Ny rov oy
I don't give a damn

Pask lowen
Happy Easter

Da yw genev ow oy gans amm
I like mine with a kiss

Nice shorts!
Would you like to dance?

Hooray, hooray for the eighth of May! It's official. It's the end of winter in Cornwall. Trees and flowers are bursting into life and people in Helston are dusting off their top hats, pinning on lily of the valley and limbering up for the furry dance on Flora Day.

Many other Cornish towns will be doing exactly the same thing this month, not just Helston. All around the world communities traditionally celebrate the end of winter with some form of ritual dance.

I remember being taught country dancing at primary school, and at the time I thought it was called country dancing because it took place on grass. In hindsight, it was clearly a repertoire of folk dances from different Countries, rather than anything to do with our proximity to the nearest city. The girls were made to wear red and white gingham gypsy skirts and neckerchiefs, and the boys wore rather disturbing white Crimplene shorts, school shirts and gingham waistcoats. I've never forgotten the dance

25

steps, and with a lot of encouragement and several glasses of red wine (**gwin rudh**) I can be persuaded to take to the dancefloor occasionally. I believe this may have happened at Lowender Peran Festival in Newquay one year – hopefully there's no video evidence. Dancing is another of those ancient traditions that helps to define Cornwall's unique cultural identity, and keeps the world capitated by all things Cornish.

My a vynn donsya
I can dance

Lavrek berr splann!
Nice shorts!

A wren ni mos dhe Hellys?
Shall we go to Helston?

Donsya y'n stret
Dancing in the street

A vynn'ta donsya genev?
Would you like to dance with me?

Pandr'a vynn'ta dhe eva?
What would you like to drink?

Gwin rudh, mar pleg
Red wine, please

I love you a thousand times more than my cows

Are you Kernewek-blind? Cornish language is not just the domain of the old Cornwall societies and Gorsedh Kernow, it's really being used. Have a look around you. I'm sat in a café in Liskeard. On my way, I saw dozens of road signs in **Kernewek** (Cornish). At one point I was stuck behind a big green recycling lorry sign-written with the words **eylgelghyans rag Kernow** (recycling for Cornwall), in my shopping bag is a bottle of **Kerensa Aval** (Apple Friendship or Apple of Love) cider vinegar, produced from Cornish apple orchards in south east Cornwall. The copy of last week's newspaper in the rack shows the date in Cornish on the front page and the music festival poster on the notice board states '**agas gweles war an treth**' (see you on the beach).

Historically, working songs were sung to help synchronise repetitive tasks on the sailing boats (**golyans skath**), in the mines (**balyow**) and on the farm (**bargen-tir**). Sea shanties are a perfect example. Singing releases endorphins in the brain, promoting a feeling of elation and pleasure, and is also known to alleviate anxiety and stress.

As a rule, we don't get many opportunities to sing at work these days. Singing folk songs whilst stacking pilchards into a barrel is probably more socially acceptable than belting-out power ballads at your desk in an open-plan office. A chap who worked in my local coffee house (**koffiji**) a few years ago used to sing (**kana**) whilst he poured, usually opera. Magical stuff, more singing baristas please. Right now, I must go to the Royal Cornwall Show.

Res yw dhymm mos dhe Dhiskwedhyans Kernow Riel | I must go to the Royal Cornwall Show

A vynn'ta mos genev? | Will you go with me?

My a'th kar milweyth moy es ow bughes
I love you a thousand times more than my cows

Pygemmys yw hemma? | How much is this?

Nyns yw unn jynn-tenna nevra lowr
One tractor is never enough

Gwren gul henna arta, nessa blydhen
Let's do that again next year

Are we there yet?

Speaking Cornish is a bit like playing that children's game where you have to avoid saying 'yes' or 'no' otherwise you're out of the game. There are no words for **yes** or **no** in the Cornish language. Imagine that.

Do you live in Cornwall? I do. Is there a harbour in the town? There is. Are you going to the beach today? I'm not. Do they understand Cornish? They don't. Should we walk the Cornish coastal path? We should. Can you see that ship? I can.

In July 1588, three ships belonging the Spanish Armada fleet were sighted off the coast of Cornwall near Saint Michael Mount. On that occasion, there was a brief skirmish off the Eddystone Rocks before the Spanish ships fled east, but there were to be many more approaches in the years that followed. On 23 July 1595, four galleys were sighted, this time they landed at Mousehole. The attacking Spanish fleet was on a reconnaissance mission from the Blavet estuary, now known as Port Louis and Lorient in Brittany. The raids were part of the ongoing conflict that tore Europe apart for almost three hundred years. France had been in a state of civil war between Catholics and Huguenots (French Protestants) for years, and both sides had called for foreign support. Shipwrecked Spanish and French sailors undoubtedly washed ashore on Cornish beaches during these invasions.

Whilst you're sitting on the beach this summer gazing at the horizon, give a thought to how much of Cornwall's history, heritage and culture is directly connected to the sea. With three hundred miles of coastline embracing a place the size of the tiny land-locked English county of Shropshire, it's no wonder.

I've always felt happier near water. There's something very grounding about looking out to sea from the safety of land, even with the threat of coastal attack. The sea – it offers a world of possibilities and a universe of unknowns. I'm slowly working my way down my bucket list, and this summer I'm going to start walking the coastal path around Cornwall. I've done several bits of it numerous times already, but I really want to start the whole route afresh and write about it as I go. I expect it will take me much longer than I plan, but like life, it's more about the journey than the destination and there's so much to see, experience and learn along the way.

A wren ni mos dhe'n treth?
Shall we go to the beach?

Mir orth henna! Gorholyon-golya!
Look at that! Sailing ships!

Esowgh war dy'gol?
Are you on holiday?

Yth eson ni ow kerdhes hyns an arvor
We're walking the coast path

Eson ni ena hwath? | Are we there yet?

Dew kans hwetek ha peswar ugens mildir dhe vos hwath
Only 296 miles to go now

Ow dewdros a shynd | My feet hurt

Yma edhomm dhymm a dhiwes | I need a drink

Ogh bryntin, diwotti! | Oh splendid, a pub!

Yeghes da | Cheers!

Skwith on ni. Eus stevel rag an nos dhywgh? |
We're tired. Do you have a room for the night?

All aboard

I missed my train this morning. It wouldn't have been so bad had I just been heading into Truro or over the bridge to Plymouth for the day, but I'm on my way to Charlottetown, Prince Edward Island, Canada. The train I'm now travelling on won't get me to Heathrow in time for my flight to Toronto, so unfortunately, I'm going to miss my connection to Charlottetown tonight.

Oh well, at least I'm sat in comfort with a latte for refreshment, power for my laptop and a mobile phone at my disposal. I'll have to make an unplanned overnight stay in Toronto but thanks to the GWR WIFI network I've already contacted Air Canada, transferred myself onto the next available flight and booked a hotel, so it could be worse. In fact, it could be a lot worse.

I'm wondering just how bad the same journey was for the Cornish families who emigrated to Prince Edward Island in the 1800s. Shipbuilding, and the mass closure of mines in Cornwall, forced thousands of people overseas in search of work and the promise of an exciting new life. Whilst many boarded ships to

Australia and South America, others headed for North America including Canada's eastern maritime provinces of New Brunswick, Nova Scotia and Prince Edward Island. PEI has a significant population of people of Cornish decent, and even has a town called Cornwall close to the capital. Those transatlantic journeys by sea, under sail, must have been absolutely terrifying, hazardous and unpredictable. My slightly delayed journey really isn't that bad.

I'm nearly at Paddington station now but I started my travels on the very beautiful Looe Valley Line this morning. Originally a mineral railway, it carried copper ore from the Caradon Moor mines down into the port of Looe where it was transferred onto boats bound for smelting plants in Hayle and Swansea. In South Wales, the empty boats would be re-filled with coal before returning to Cornwall. When the mines closed, it was converted into a passenger railway, linking Looe with the London to Penzance mainline at Liskeard, and making Looe a destination of choice for the affluent Victorian holiday-maker.

There's something magical about traveling to and from Cornwall by train. Maybe it's the change in landscape or just the fact that you can see the coastline. Crossing the Tamar on Brunel's iconic railway bridge always feels special, especially on the way *back* into Cornwall. I look forward to doing that next week. See you soon Cornwall (**dha weles yn skon Kernow**).

Hedh an tren na!
Hold that train!

Py kay rag Pennsans, mar pleg?
Which platform for Penzance, please?

A wra an tren ma hedhi yn Bosvenegh?
Does this train stop at Bodmin?

Gav dhymm, mes henn yw ow hador, dell dybav
Excuse me, but I think that's my seat

Eus esedhow gesys?
Are there any seats left?

My a yll gweles an mor
I can see the sea

Bydh war an aswa | Mind the gap

An tren yw ugens mynysenn yn diwedhes
The train is twenty minutes late

Toknys mar pleg | Tickets please

Do you come here often?

I found myself speaking Cornish in some unusual circumstances recently, not just in class but whilst ordering food in a café in Truro, on a train coming back from London (when a conversation erupted amongst passengers further up the carriage about whether Cornish is still spoken or not), on stage and in radio interviews. I've even started flirting in Cornish. I had no idea speaking Cornish was going to be such an asset to dating.

Developing and maintaining a long-distance relationship is a challenge, particularly when you live and work full-time in Cornwall. It takes a fair amount of thought and a huge amount of planning. I'm not a character from Poldark though, so I don't have to sit at my writing desk to pen carefully considered love letters to the object of my desire hundreds of miles away. Neither do I need to spend several tormented days wondering whether they've been received, and if so, what his response might be.

Thankfully, digital 'apps' now provide almost-immediate channels of communication with my friends and family around the world. Not nearly so romantic, but lots of fun and no guess-work involved. A couple of weeks ago, my version of sitting down to write a love letter was a spontaneous decision to record a short video of myself speaking *sweet nothings* in Cornish.

In my head, I imagined a scene akin to one from the 1942 film *Casablanca*. You know, cigarette smoke and train smog, sultry lighting, monotone cinematic perfection, beautiful hats and perfect make-up (and that's just the men). Ingrid Bergman whispering sexily in a vaguely foreign accent, lots of pouting and introspective gazing towards the horizon.

In reality, I was dressed for a Cornish summer in a beanie hat and bright yellow waterproof coat, holding my iPhone at arm's length, camera in selfie mode, trying to navigate the quayside safely at the same time as looking at the camera and speaking in Cornish. It took several attempts. In the meantime, mizzle had soaked my phone screen so much that I couldn't stop it recording. Not exactly a perfume-infused, hand-written billet-doux, but my efforts were appreciated nevertheless. It is, after all, the thought that counts.

Dos omma yn fenowgh?
Come here often?

Pyth yw dha hanow? | What's your name?

Ow hanow yw Ingrid | My name is Ingrid

Pandra vynn'ta dhe eva?
What would you like to drink?

My a vynnsa gin, mar pleg
I would like gin, please

Yeghes da | Cheers

Hemm a wel avel dalleth kowethegeth deg
This looks like the beginning of a beautiful friendship

Dhe by eur a dhiberth dha dren?
What time does your train leave?

Eth eur | Eight o'clock

Ha'n termyn ow passya | As time goes by

Ny vynnav mos tre
I don't want to go home

Gwar-e arta, Sam
Play it again Sam

Y fydh pub prys Kammbronn dhyn
We'll always have Camborne

My a vydh lowen
I shall be happy

Fatel leverir … yn kernewek?
How do you say … in Cornish?

Everything stops for tea

What is it about gazing into a cup of tea that instantly calms any situation? I've often wondered what non-tea drinkers do in times of crisis.

I remember my very first cup of tea. I was sixteen and I'd just started art college. Pete, one of the lads in my newly formed friendship group, lived close to the college so we often popped round to his house before or after (and sometimes during) lectures. He had three brothers and his parents were the salt of the earth so Pete's house was always brimming with people. Tea was a big thing in their household. They had a massive, dark wood kitchen table surrounded by benches. That table become the nerve centre of college life.

On our first visit to Pete's house, after introductions were complete, we sat at the table and watched Pete's mum pour six mugs of tea from a huge, red teapot. At that point I probably should have owned up to the fact that I didn't drink tea, but in those days I was painfully shy (yes, really) and couldn't bring myself to say the words. I was a coffee drinker, but Pete's house wasn't the sort of house where you drank coffee. So, in complete silence I accepted the mug of steaming tea, laced it with milk and sugar and sipped it, very slowly.

By the time I could see the bottom of the mug I was hooked, on life and on tea. It was a life-changing moment.

Tea seems to have featured heavily in my life ever since. Bad days and good days all start and end with tea. My morning begins with at least two cups (don't bother trying to speak to me before my second cup). Tea is very much part of Cornish life. I've spent many lazy afternoons drooling over cakey tea and cream teas. Tea has been present at all my important life milestones. Many difficult conversations have started, and finished, with *"I'll put the kettle on!"* Staring with unfocussed eyes into a mug of steaming tea seems to help reflect on what's important.

For me, November is always a time for reflection. The nights are drawing in and winter is upon us. In Cornish, November is **mis-Du** which translates as 'dark month'.

As Remembrance Day approaches I've been thinking about the lost gardeners of the Heligan estate who died in active service during World War One, and one gardener in particular, William Guy. His extraordinary story is captured in a beautiful book called *'A Song for Will'*, written by Hilary Robinson, and illustrated by Martin Impey and for which I wrote music to accompany the book launch.

Songwriting is always an emotional experience but writing music for *'A Song for Will'* was very special. I spent a lot of time at Heligan doing research and was lucky enough to be able to look around the house itself. In my mind, I could see a young William Guy and his sweetheart sat at a huge kitchen table 'below stairs', drinking tea with the rest of the estate staff.

I have a dark wood kitchen table of my own now, around which my teenage children sit with their friends putting the world to rights. Watching my fifteen-year-old son make tea in our vintage Woods Wear Beryl teapot and pour it for our house guests is a thing of beauty. As a family, we meet at that table every evening and share our respective days. For a few minutes time stops, whilst we stir the pot and wait for the magic to happen. It's true, everything does stop for tea.

Pandra vynn'ta dhe eva?
What would you like to drink?

My a vynnsa eva te, mar pleg
I would like tea, please

Prys te yw | It's tea time

Puptra a hedh rag te
Everything stops for tea

Leth kynsa po te kynsa?
Milk first or tea first?

Moy a de, Pronter?
More tea, Vicar?

Nyns yw ow hanafas te
It's not my cup of tea

Henn yw ogas kemmys devnydh avel pott te a joklet
That's about as much use as a chocolate teapot

Mis-Du | November

Jingle Bells

December is the time of year when we bring a little piece of the outdoors, indoors. Trees, holly, ivy and mistletoe all make their way into our homes – beautiful, vibrant green foliage in an otherwise dark and gloomy month. December (**mis-Kevardhu** in Cornish) hails the start of winter in the Northern Hemisphere, where the shortest day and the longest night are marked by the winter solstice. A custom called *Chalking of the Mock*, is performed around *Montol*, or the winter solstice, in Cornwall. The mock (a yule log) is chalked – a stick man is drawn on the wood. As part of the ceremony, the appointed *Lord of Misrule* declares, *"According to our tradition this represents the end of the old and the beginning of the new"*. The Mock is then burnt.

Who can resist staring blankly into the dancing flames of a burning log or sitting quietly by candlelight? There's something mesmerising about a flickering flame. A blazing yule log is thought to create the perfect festive ambience in many cultures. It's easy to forget that many Christmas rituals have their roots in old Celtic traditions. The English word December is derived from the Latin word *decem*, meaning ten, as it used to be the tenth month of the Roman calendar. Anglo-Saxons referred to December as Yule time or Yuletide.

We've also been decking our halls with boughs of holly for centuries. Hanging a holly wreath outside the house dates back to pre-Christian times when they were believed to ward off evil spirits. In Celtic tradition, the holly tree was revered as a powerful and magical plant and a traditional Cornish Christmas tree is a **kelynnen** or holly bush, rather than a conifer.

Whatever rites and rituals you plan to practice over the festive period, if you're sending greetings cards to friends and family try your hand at writing them in Cornish. Here are a few phrases to help you craft the perfect message in Kernewek.

Dhe | To

Gorhemynadow an Seson | Season's Greetings

Nadelik Lowen | Happy Christmas

Gans kerensa | With love

Dhyworth | From

I've found that putting sticky notes on everyday items showing their name in Cornish is a great way to familiarise yourself with new words. I don't condone slapping sticky notes on passing angels or unsuspecting reindeer, but it's a very useful *aide memoire* – I've even been known to label my children.

El | Angel

Karow Ergh | Reindeer

Den Ergh | Snowman

Gwedhen Nadelik | Christmas Tree

Kantol | Candle

Kelyn | Holly

Lodrik | Stocking

Podin Nadelik | Christmas Pudding

Ro | Present

Rudhek | Robin

Steren | Star

Tas Nadelik | Father Christmas

Tesen Nadelik | Christmas Cake

Ughelvar | Mistletoe

Pastigow brewgig
Mince pies

It's likely that Christmas songs will be unavoidable this month so have some fun singing Jingle Bells in Kernewek too. **Nadelik Lowen ha Bledhen Nowydh Da** (happy Christmas and a good new year).

Klegh a sen! Klegh a sen!
Jingle bells! Jingle bells!

Ow seni oll a-dro
Jingle all the way

Ass yw brav dhe lewya
Oh what fun, it is to ride

Yn draylel unn vargh heb to
In a one-horse open sleigh

Cheese please Louise

Hands up, who ate too much over the festive season? Just out of curiosity, is your fridge full of cheese? Mine is still rammed with unopened speciality cheeses; the ones containing fruit and chillies, hard cheese, soft cheese, crumbly cheese, cheeses wrapped in nettles and small smelly cheeses in boxes.

Charles de Gaulle is quoted as saying, *"How can anyone govern a nation that has two hundred and forty-six different kinds of cheese?"*. Cornwall has a fair few unique and award-winning cheeses of its own, which I seem to overbuy every Christmas in anticipation of a hoard of hungry friends dropping in for some sort of impromptu cheese-fest. Strangely, that has never happened, but let's face it, cheese is fabulous.

The subject of cheese has provided hours of fun in my Cornish language classes, which take place over lunch in a coffee shop in Truro. We often ask each other **"Eus keus genes?",** pronounced *errs kerrs genez*. It means *"do you have cheese?"* but the literal translation is *"is* *there cheese with you?"*. The response is usually **"Eus. Yma keus genev."**, *"There is. There is cheese with me"*.

I love cheese, in an omelette with a hunk of bread (**bara**), melted *au gratin* style on vegetables or just with a juicy apple (**aval**). They say that if you have cheese in the house, you'll never go hungry. Whether you're a feta fanatic, gorgonzola glutton or an aged-cheddar addict, cheese offers something for everyone. Burgers, pasties, sandwiches, sauces, salads, picnics, wraps, potatoes and pasta – all rely on cheese for embellishment.

Next time you peer into your fridge, give a little nod of appreciation to the cheese languishing there. You'll be grateful for it one day (pun intended).

Pandr'a vynn'ta dybri? | What would you like to eat?

Keus ragov, mar pleg | Cheese for me, please

Da yw genev keus hag aval y'n kettermyn
I like cheese and apple at the same time

Eus Brie Kernewek genes?
Do you have Cornish Brie?

Splann yw Yarg Kernewek
Cornish Yarg is splendid

Keus, mar pleg, Louise
Cheese, please, Louise

Keus yw sand an jydh
Dish of the day, is cheese

Da yw genev keus
I like cheese

If your seasonal indulgences are anything like mine, losing weight will be top of your list of new year resolutions. If so, you might want to consider giving up the following:

Tesen | Cake

Kresigow | Crisps

Pasti | Pasty

Tesen gales | Biscuit

Choklet | Chocolate

Pysk hag asklos | Fish and chips

Korev | Beer

Gwin rudh | Red wine

Dowr tomm Alban | Whisky

According to research, eighty percent of new year resolutions are said to fail by February, which means that twenty percent might succeed. Popular resolutions include taking more exercise, quitting smoking, spending more time with loved ones and learning a new skill. So, what about adding learning to speak Cornish to your list of new year resolutions?

Learning a second language is good for you. Research into the effects of learning and speaking languages shows that being bilingual improves cognitive skills and overall brain function. It stimulates the hippocampus and areas of the cerebral cortex, and slows brain-aging. Adults who speak multiple languages are more likely to have higher general intelligence as a result. Isn't that motivation enough to learn Kernewek? If not, do it because it's part of Cornwall's unique heritage or just because it's fun (and sometimes involves cheese).

Get your coat, you've pulled

How are those New Year resolutions going? Well done if you're still fully committed in February.

What does February have in store? For me, it's all about frosty mornings, clear skies, half-term mayhem, Brittany, my birthday and talking of commitment; Valentine's Day.

Gone are the days of embroidered hand-crafted declarations of love containing pieces of human hair (probably a good thing). Now, it's all about instant digital messages accompanied by a few abbreviated words and suggestive emojis. Put the romance back into Valentine's Day this year by sending your sweetheart a message in Cornish language.

I was walking my dog up near the Cheesewring on Bodmin Moor recently. It was snowing lightly and bitterly cold. It got me thinking about life on Caradon Moor hundreds of years ago, well before central heating, instant hot water and proper roads. I was thinking about Daniel Gumb – a stone cutter, born in 1703 and who lived in a cave on Stowes Hill for over fifty years.

With an open fire and a slab of granite for its roof, these days we'd call Daniel Gumb's cave an eco-house. It would be one of those unique homes that feature in *George Clark's Amazing Spaces* described as a small subterranean bolthole. It must have been reasonably cosy though as he had a wife and several children there.

Rag ow melder | For my sweetheart

Dydh Sen Valentin Lowen | Happy Saint Valentine's Day

A vyn'ta mos yn-mes genev? | Will you go out with me?

My a'th kar | I love you

A vyn'ta demedhi genev? | Will you marry me?

Gans oll ow herensa | With all my love

Dhyworth estemyor kevrinek | From a mystery admirer

A wre'ta dos omma yn fenowgh?
Do you come here often?

Kyrgh dha gota, ty re dennas!
Get your coat, you've pulled!

Off with his head!

Whilst trying to work out how to translate the idiom 'mad as a March hare' into Cornish, I started thinking about children's stories and nursery rhymes.

There are so many gruesome tales recited by children, in cheerfully ignorance of their meaning. In *Three Blind Mice* for example, the rodents represent noblemen who were convicted of plotting against Queen Mary (the farmer's wife). Although, according to the history books, they were spared the carving knife and burned at the stake instead. Bonus.

Ring A Ring O' Roses is well known for depicting the symptoms of the Black Death, which was responsible for the demise of millions of people in the fourteenth Century wiping out sixty per cent of Europe's population in the process. So, it's less about skipping daintily around a rosebush suffering from hay fever and more about the common symptoms of the plague: ring-shaped skin rashes and sneezing. People were believed to fill their pockets with sweet smelling flowers and herbs to cover up the bad smells, hence the term 'a pocket full of posies'. Most of the UK seems to have succumbed to cold viruses at the moment so I hope you're surviving the dark winter months.

As March arrives, the days lengthen we venture outdoors again. This month we'll be busy spring-cleaning and behaving slightly strangely, like wild hares.

Mar vuskok avel skovarnek yn mis Meurth
As mad as a March hare

Mar veri avel hok
As merry as a hawk

Re bo dibennys!
Off with his head!

Shakespeare used the phrase 'off with his head' many times in his plays. For example, in *Henry VI Part III*, Queen Margaret says, *"Off with his head, and set it on York gates; so York may overlook the town of York."*
Lewis Carroll is probably the best-known user of the phrase however, when he included it in *Alice's Adventures in Wonderland* in 1865. Whilst the playing cards argue and fight noisily for hedgehogs, the Queen of Hearts stomps around shrieking *"off with their heads"*

every two minutes. The mad march hare is also synonymous with the Mad Hatter, who also appears in *Alice's Adventures in Wonderland.*

Baa Baa Black Sheep is thought to have something to do with the Great Custom tax on wool from 1275 and is loaded with political content.

Mary Had a Little Lamb is possibly one of the few nursery rhymes with a clear and innocuous origin however. A poem written by Sarah Josepha Hale in 1830, it was inspired by a girl named Mary Sawyer who took her pet lamb to school.

Here's the first verse in Cornish:

Maria hi a's tevo oen | Mary had a little lamb

Mar wynn avel an ergh | It's fleece was white as snow

Hag yn pub le may kerdhi-hi | And everywhere that Mary went

An oen eth war hy lergh | The lamb was sure to go

It's not a perfect translation due to the rhyming form and the meter of the poem, but the context is roughly the same, much like all translations of English into Cornish.

How do you eat an elephant?

I started running recently, which can only be a good thing as I'm rather partial to a certain brand of small, cream-filled chocolate egg. I've never been a runner. I've always preferred swimming, diving and yoga. Even when I was young, I never really ran. Track and field wasn't my thing at school (although I was pretty nifty at the high jump), and cross-country running filled me with dread. Hauling my lethargic teenage body around the perimeter of a muddy school field in the freezing cold wasn't my idea of fun.

I've always secretly wanted to run though, I just never believed I could, and that's half the battle it seems. The running club in my town has gone from strength to strength in recent years. On Tuesday and Thursday evenings, the streets are awash with brightly coloured Lycra as runners of all shapes, sizes and abilities pound the quayside in pursuit of increased fitness. Along with speaking Cornish, learning to run was one of my bucket list items. I enrolled on a beginner's *Couch to 5k* programme in January and (unbelievably) we're well over half way through the course and I'm managing to keep up. But how do you run five kilometres when the furthest you've ever sprinted is from the car to the front door to avoid the rain? One step at a time. It's so important to build up to something in stages, set achievable and realistic goals – and just start. The App on my phone helps me see what I've achieved, breaking down training sessions and routes into manageable chunks. It's amazing how quickly my fitness is improving. I'm starting to believe I **can** run.

It's the same with learning to speak Cornish, things are starting to make sense and responses are becoming intuitive. The more words I learn, the easier it becomes to make sentences and hold short conversations. I'm starting to believe I **can** speak Cornish fluently. How do you learn a new language? One word at a time with it.

Language is intrinsic to culture. A means of communicating, but also of preserving values, beliefs and customs. When languages disappear, part of that culture dies with it.

So, how do you eat an elephant? One small piece at a time. A short walk, and two new Cornish words a day will make all the difference, to your health and to Cornish culture. When many people do that at the same time, you start to change the world. You just have to start.

One of my favourite inspirational quotes is from W H Murray, who said *"Whatever you can do, or dream you can do, begin it. Boldness has genius, power and magic in it."*

Whatever's on your bucket list – be bold and begin. What are you waiting for? A thousand-mile journey begins with a single step.

My a yll ponya | I can run

A vynn'ta ponya genev?
Would you like to run with me?

Fatla genes? | How are you?

Ow dewdros a shynd, mes yn poynt da
My feet hurt, but in good health

Pyth yw henna? | What is that?

Olifans yw | It's an elephant

Ev yw ow howeth | He is my friend

A bleth os ta devedhys?
Where do you come from?

Devedhys ov a Eynda | I come from India

A wre'ta kewsel Kernewek hwath?
Can you speak Cornish yet?

Nebes | A little

Dance and feast and sing

On or around the eighth of May each year, one of Cornwall's oldest customs, the Furry Dance takes place in Helston. It marks the Feast of Saint Michael, and is better known as Flora Day. A celebration of the passing of winter and the arrival of spring, the day of dancing and feasting starts at 7am prompt with the 'morning dance'.

Forming part of the Flora Day festivities is the Hal-an-Tow, a kind of mystery play performed at seven locations around town, starting at Saint John's Bridge. The Hal-an-Tow pageant tells the story of Helston and includes characters such as Friar Tuck, Robin Hood, St. George, St. Michael and the devil. It also contains disparaging references to Spaniards referring directly to the Spanish raid on Mousehole, Newlyn and Penzance in 1595.

The Flora Day festivities continue with the midday dance, when eighty beautifully turned-out couples wind their way around the town; the men in top hats and tails, and the women in their finest dresses.

Dancers, bandsmen and those who are Helston-born wear *Lily of the Valley* – gentlemen wearing it on the left (with the flowers pointing upwards) and the ladies wearing it (upside down) on the right.

Cornish people love a good feast. What's not to like about dancing, eating, drinking and chasing away unwanted and negative influences. All good, I say.

The weather may have taken a well-overdue turn for the better recently but remember, *"Ne'er cast a clout 'til May be out"* – basically, keep your vest on until June ... or at least until the Hawthorn's in bloom.

Res yw dhymm mos dhe Hellys
I must go to Helston

A vynn'ta mos genev?
Will you go with me?

An ethves mis Me | The eight of May

Gool | Festival or feast

Donsya y'n stret
Dancing in the street

A vynn'ta donsya genev?
Would you like to dance with me?

Py eur yw?
What time is it?

Hanter wosa eth eur yw
It's half past eight

Hanter-dydh yw | It's Midday

My a yll kana yn Kernewek
I can sing in Cornish

My a yll donsya | I can dance

Kler ha splann an korev
Clear and bright the ale

Rudh ha gwynn an ros
Red and white the rose

Onan, dew, tri, peswar, pymp
One, two, three, four, five

Follow the sun, follow your heart

In a month when holidaymakers from all over the world make their annual pilgrimage to Kernow, I've been wondering how many millions of people have arrived on Cornish shores since the beginning of time.

All those explorers and invaders, traders and merchants, farmers and fishermen, missionaries and pilgrims who made epic journeys by sea and on foot. Why did they come? What did they find? A matter of survival for many; those early settlers created new communities, introduced different cultures and made Cornwall what it is today.

Summer stopovers in the region tend to be less hazardous nowadays. Instead of treacherous voyages by ship, visitors arrive in relative comfort by car, train or air. We're all still adventurers at heart though; hunter-gatherers, clansmen, and tribes people. We all love a feast and a festival, a gathering, an excursion or a short trip to a special place. Cornwall is certainly special. An extraordinary place to the West where the land ends, the sun sets and the magic happens. Perhaps we have a deep-rooted primal instinct to migrate and gather here once a year – like birds flying south for the winter, following the sun.

Kernow seems always to have been a place of pilgrimage. When the saints arrived on Cornish soil between 500 and 600 AD they risked everything to bring Christianity here. Saint Piran's own story is a good example. Legend has it that the heathen Irish tied him to a millstone and rolled it over the edge of a cliff into a stormy sea. The water, however, immediately fell calm and he floated over the sea, landing safely on the sandy beach of Perranzabuloe.

If you enjoy walking, the *Cornish Celtic Way* is a pilgrimage trail covering one hundred and twenty-five miles between Saint German's and Saint Michael's Mount. Incorporating sixty miles of coastal path and two established pilgrimage routes, the Saints' Way and Saint Michael's Way, the *Cornish Celtic Way* invites you to walk in the footsteps of saints and visit sites of special significance along the way, such as Celtic crosses, standing stones, holy wells and churches.

It's hard to believe, but not everyone who ends up in Cornwall actually wants to be here. Shipwreck victims, asylum seekers and prisoners for example. So next time you're staring out of the window of a packed train winding its way from Paddington to Penzance, or crawling along the A30 in a hot car, spare a thought for those early travelers to the Cornish coast.

Holyewgh an howl, holyewgh agas kolonn
Follow the sun, follow your heart

Kewgh gans agas teylu ha kewgh dhe'n howlsedhes
Go with your families and go west

Eson ni ena hwath?
Are we there yet?

Esowgh war dy'gol?
Are you on holiday?

A wren ni mos dhe'n treth?
Shall we go to the beach?

Mir orth henna! Gorholyon-golya!

Look at that! Sailing ships!
Kewgh dhe howlsedhes, pergherinyon
Go west, pilgrims

Yth eson ni ow kerdhes hyns an arvor
We're walking the coast path

Agas gweles war an treth
See you on the beach

The Great Escape

I've been rediscovering Cornwall this summer, seeing it from a whole new perspective – from astride a motorbike. Wandering through Truro one Saturday afternoon in July, I fell in love with a devilishly handsome Mutt Mongrel in the window of Clique Customs in Kenwyn Street.

Looking like it belonged in a Sixties Steve McQueen movie, the matt-black retro-styled machine winked seductively at me as I walked past. Ten days later it was parked outside my house.

I went into town for a set of mandolin strings, and went home with a new lease of life.

The first time I went out on the Mutt, I rode tentatively through the crowded streets of Looe. Nervous after such a long break from motorcycling, I was eager not to collide with any unsuspecting holidaymakers. Creeping along at less than 10mph in first gear, slipping the clutch and revving the engine, I started to relax. It felt great. The bike's low throaty growl bounced back at me from the granite walls of Looe's narrow streets, turning heads on every corner. So, I'm back on two wheels. And, *on any Sunday* and on warm evenings over the past few weeks I've been escaping, taking the *long way 'round* through the backroads of East Cornwall, leaning into hairpins again and enjoying Kernow from a completely different angle. It's like seeing your commuter route from the top deck of a bus for the first time, instead of from the driver's seat of your car.

I've discovered roads, bridges and hamlets I never knew existed – all within a five mile of home. Even the journeys I've been taking every day for the past ten years I now see in a different light. I've become more aware of my surroundings.

When you're on a bike (pedal-powered or engine-powered) unprotected from the elements; the noise, smell and light of a place smacks you between the eyes – literally. You really don't have to go very far to remind yourself how special Cornwall is.

What a pleasure it is to discover new places right on your doorstep and fall in love with your surroundings all over again. Life on the open road. I highly recommend it.

Lots of the places I've discovered recently have traditional Cornish names – you know, the ones that start with **Tre**, **Pol** or **Pen**.

Many Cornish place names start with Tre; Trebetherick, Trelissick, Trenant. **Tre** means homestead or farm.

Pol, as in Polbathic, Polzeath, Polperro and Polruan means pool.

Pen, as in Penzance, Pendennis, Penryn and Pentire means head, headland or the end of something.

Other common prefixes in Cornish place names are **Porth**, meaning harbour or bay as in Porthleven, Perranporth and Porthtowan; and **Lan** like in Lanhydrock, Landrake, and Lanteglos which means sacred place.

Whether your wheels have an engine or not, venture out this autumn, get up to speed with your local area, head for the hills, feel the wind in your hair and fall in love with Cornwall all over again.

I never did get the mandolin strings. I'd better get tuned up!

Yw semlant ow thin bras war an jynn-diw ros ma?
Does my bum look big on this motorbike?

Yw da genes jynnow-diw ros?
Do you like motorbikes?

Gwren ni skapya!
Let's escape!

Kar vy, kar ow diw ros
Love me, love my bike

An Diank Vras
The Great Escape

Gwrys yn Kernow
Made in Cornwall

Onan hag Oll
One and All

Di wros yw gwell ages peder
Two wheels are better than four

kynnyav yw
It's autumn

Make the change

For as long as I can remember, October has been a significant month for me. A time of transition, when projects come to an end and others start, when big life-events happen and when major moves take place. I've often met influential people in October and made trips that have turned out to be pivotal moments in my life.

There's something about October that I really like. It's my favourite month of the year. It's a time of change. Even time itself changes in the UK this month, as clocks go back an hour bringing dark, misty mornings.

I love the clarity of autumn sunshine and the coolness of the air; they herald a period of rest and recuperation. It really is the end of the summer now. Those beautiful warm days in September were a bonus. A nesting instinct is kicking in, a desire to stock-up, lock-down and hibernate like animals getting ready for the winter.

On chilly October mornings, you realise how many spiders there are in the world. Dew-heavy cobwebs in hedgerows, on foliage, clinging to fences and strung to car wing mirrors. Those savvy little arachnids make a dash for the warmth of the house too, appearing in bathtubs and other visible places. Those spiders and their silky webs were there all along of course, we just couldn't see them until October brought them into sharp focus. It does that. We start thinking about the year that's been. It's nearly over and what have we achieved?

A time for contemplation, planning and preparation and a time of plenty too. We pickle and preserve. We harvest berries, fruits, nuts and seeds in abundance, and brightly coloured gourds, squash and pumpkins adorn the displays of road-side farm shops.

Nothing says October better than the smooth, oily surface of a *conker* peeping out from the prickly green case of a fallen horse chestnut fruit. Oh, the simple joy of discovering a freshly fallen conker!

If you're a keen gardener, there are loads of jobs to get stuck into outdoors in October. It's a great time to plant forget-me-nots, pansies and wallflowers and the perfect month to bury spring bulbs or turn over your vegetable patch. Make sure you leave seed-heads on plants to provide food for birds over the winter, and let leaves stay where they fall to give shelter and protection to wildlife and insects.

Create a little eco-haven for wildlife in your garden. Pile a few bits of wood, logs or tree branches in a shady corner. After a while, it will attract all manner of insects and provide a safe place for toads and hedgehogs to spend the winter. Your wood pile will eventually sprout fungi – nature's own recycling system – which turns dead wood back into soil. Everything changes.

Mis Hedra yw
It's October

Prys yw
It's time

Yma kevnis y'n kibel
There's a spider in the bath

Drog yw genev kevnis | I don't like spiders

A siowgh neppyth tamm dyffrans?
Fancy something a bit different?

My a vynnsa pompyon, mar pleg
I would like a pumpkin, please

Gwren ni neyja soth rag gwav
Let's fly south for the winter

**Mar ny ethewgh bythkweth dhe'n Gool Ester
Aberfala, hwi a wra kavos delit bras**
If you've never been to Falmouth Oyster Festival, you're
in for a treat

Gwren ni gwari conkers
Let's play conkers

Names on a wall

For the past couple of years, I've been working on a joint project with the Lost Gardens of Heligan involving the creation of new music to commemorate the fallen soldiers of World War One, in particular, the lost gardeners of the Heligan estate.

My musical partner, Sam Kelly and I produced an EP for the project, one song for which was sung in Cornish language. The songs tell the story of the Heligan gardeners, who signed their names on the wall of the Thunderbox Room above the date August 1914, before they went off to fight for their country. Their departure marked the beginning of years of decline for the gardens at Heligan and it wasn't until 1990 when the Thunderbox Room was excavated that their names were discovered and the story came to light. The wall bearing the gardeners' names is now recognised by the Imperial War Museum as a 'Living Memorial'.

Candy Smit, archivist for The Lost Gardens of Heligan said, *"There were twenty-two outdoor staff on the books at Heligan in August 1914 – and only half remained a year later; little more than a third by 1917. So far, we have researched the histories of thirteen Heligan men who went to war, and only four survived. Their fading signatures are a constant reminder of the ultimate sacrifice that was made and of our responsibility to them to find another way today. Tanya Brittain's poignant and well-crafted lyric writing and Sam Kelly's stunning vocals perfectly capture the essence and mood of the story."*

Each November we remember the fallen as we read their names on monuments, plaques and walls worldwide. I wanted the sentiment of the title track, *Names On A Wall,* to be timeless and universal even though it's essentially about the men from Heligan, so I'm delighted that *Names On A Wall* is now widely sung by military choirs.

A wre'ta kewsel Kernewek hwath?
Can you speak Cornish yet?

Nebes | A little

Res yw dhymm mos dhe Lowender Peran
I must go to Lowender Peran

A vynn'ta mos genev?
Will you go with me?

A bleth os ta devedhys?
Where do you come from?

Devedhys ov a Gembra
I come from Wales

A wre'ta dos omma yn fenowgh?
Do you come here often?

Pub prys | All the time

My a vynn amontya yn Kernewek
I can count in Cornish

Ny rov oy | I don't give a damn

Onan, dew, tri, peswar, pymp
One, two, three, four, five

Mis-Du | November (dark month)

Ni a wra aga hofhe | We will remember them

Henwyn orth fos | Names on a wall

Put a lid on it

I'm currently surrounded by dozens of boxes. Cardboard packing boxes, plastic storage boxes, oddly shaped packages containing unwanted household items I've sold online and parcels containing gifts, wrapped and ready for Santa's arrival.

When I was a child, I had a recurring dream about packages wrapped up with brown paper and string. It wasn't a nightmare, just a vivid dream I used to have every Christmas without fail. In my dream, the boxes would appear like music notes on a giant stave. I've no idea what it meant, but music and boxes have always been important to me. I love a box. Harbingers of surprise and change. There's certainly lots changing in my world right now. I'm moving house – definitely one of the most stressful things you can do in life.

Maybe it's something you do when you get to a certain age but I'm now shedding instead of accumulating. I've sold a lot of the things I've carted around for years, recycled a load more and the rest I've boxed up ready for my forthcoming house move.

I remember my mum doing the same thing, at a similar age. She started distributing family heirlooms to my sister and myself. Keepsakes, all of them worthless apart from the sentimental value they carry and the fond memories they evoke. It's always exciting to open a box that's been stored away for a long time.

There's something cathartic about sorting through your belongings and deciding which things to hold on to, and what to let go of forever. It's particularly poignant doing it in the lead up to Christmas. A time for giving and receiving, for remembering the good things and putting a lid on everything else.

Talking of lids, where do you stand on minces pies? Open-topped pies with snowflake-shaped shortcrust lids seem to be popular this year. Personally, I prefer a full lid with crispy granulated sugar glaze (like my mum bakes) rather than the traditional dusting of icing sugar.

RESAYT   RECIPE

Pastigow Brewgik   ## Mince Pies

Devnydhyow   **Ingredients**
Bleus 110g   Flour 110g
Blonek 50g   Blonek 50g
Holan   Salt
Dowr   Water
Brewgik 500g   Mince Meat 500g

Yma edhom a ...   **You will need ...**
Mantol   Scales
Bolla   Bowl
Kollel   Knife
Forgh   Fork
Lo   Spoon
Rolbren   Rolling Pin
Trehellow toos   Pastry Cutters
Servyer pastik   Pie Tray
Forn   Oven

1   Put the **bleus** in a **bolla**
2   Cut the **blonek** into little pieces and rub into the **bleus**
    until you have the mix like breadcrumbs
3   Add the pinch of **holan**
4   Add the **dowr** bit by bit and mix with a **forgh**
5   Get your hands in there and knead until you have dough
6   Roll out with a **rolbren**
7   Use the **trehellow toos** to cut six circles, place in the
    servyer pastik
8   Fill the pies with the **brewgik**
9   Top with pastry circles
10 Bake in a **forn** at $180^{\circ c}$ for 30 minutes

Letters that changed the world

I'm sitting at an old wooden desk, a pad of smooth white writing paper set out in front of me at a slight angle. In my right hand is a fountain pen, topped-up with royal blue ink and the nib tested a few times on the blotting paper to my right. In the same daydream, I'm thinking about the person I'm about to write to, my pen is poised above the top left hand corner of the paper and I'm ready to capture whatever thoughts and feelings come to mind. *"Dearest ..."*

It's a romantic ideal. A sentimental throwback to the days before electronic communication, but there's something magical about a handwritten envelope dropping through your letterbox. It has weight and impact. You can hear it fall to the floor. It contains something touched by the writer, by a human. The same human who purchased the stamp and placed the letter in the red pillar box at the end of their road. When you open it, it makes a noise. It's physical, it has energy; as if part of the person who wrote it is inside the envelope. What a treat it is to know that someone took the time to write a letter to *you*, to focus on *you* to the exclusion of all other distractions however briefly and to go to the trouble of posting it by hand. Very different to opening an email, or receiving a text containing a *thumbs-up* emoji.

A handwritten letter is a unique, private and personal record of what was important, current and topical in that moment. A time capsule. A keepsake from another lifetime.

Author Simon Sebag Montefiore, has just published his latest book, *Written in History: Letters that Changed the World* in which he shares and celebrates one hundred fascinating letters of world history, culture and personal lives. Some are inspiring, some shocking; some are exquisite works of literature, others brutal; many are erotic and others heart-breaking but they give us a greater understanding of how events in history affect how we live now.

Last year, I contributed to the **Dasserghi Kernewek** (Reviving Cornish) project by adding Cornish language narrative to a Heritage Lottery funded film, the Story of Henry Jenner. Jenner (1848-1934) campaigned for Cornwall to be recognised as a Celtic nation and to establish Kernewek as a living, spoken language. Commissioned by the Cornish Language Office in conjunction with the Cornwall Records Office and the

Institute of Cornish Studies, the film tells the tale of the remarkable resurrection of Cornish language, and the part Henry Jenner played in its revival. The film includes dialogue from novice Cornish speakers like me, people who continue to support the revival.

The Dasserghi Kernewek project also included an exhibition of the letters of Henry Jenner; irreplaceable, original documents, handwritten by Jenner himself in both Cornish and English. Letters that are vital to the evolution and longevity of Kernewek as a living language. Letters that changed the world.

Put pen to paper this year. Let a loved one know you're thinking of them (throw in a Cornish sentence or two). Make someone's day. Change the world.

Pyth yw hemma? | What is this?

Yma lyther war an strel
There's a letter on the mat

Yw hemma dha drgiva?
What is your address?

Res yw dhymm mos dhe'n lytherva
I must go to the Post Office

My a vynnsa kavos stamp, mar pleg
I would like a stamp, please

Lyther | Letter

Kist lytherow | Letterbox

Kesskrifans | Correspondence

Dhornskrifans | Written by hand

Hem yw dha dhornskrifans? | Is this your handwriting?

Letherwas | Postman

Pluven | Pen

Paper skrifa | Writing paper

Dhe | To

Gans oll ow herensa | With all my love

Lytherow a janj an bys | Letters change the world

Flipping heck

I can't believe it's pancake day again. Honestly, it just crêped up on me. I love a pancake. As kids, we had them with fresh oranges and loads of granulated sugar. Mum gave each of us half an orange to squeeze over the wonderful disk-shaped delights. It was a team event, a human production line, mum preparing the batter and warming the frying pan, dad then taking over as chief-fryer and flipper, and my sister and I delivering pancakes to the table in strict rotation.

For my family, pancakes were a once-a-year thing, we would eat and eat, until the huge batter-jug ran dry, until the last oddly shaped half-pancake was consumed and until our bellies hurt. Ironically, in the US and France, pancake day is known as Mardi Gras, which translates as Fat Tuesday.

Pancake Day is traditionally celebrated on Shrove Tuesday, when the dish is made to use up all perishable items before the Christian period of Lent – a time of contemplation and going without pleasures. But we've been enjoying pancakes since the Stone Age. A simple flat griddle-cake, made of flour, curdled milk and eggs, pancakes have been a stalwart diet item for thousands of years. Shrove Tuesday may have Celtic pagan origins and have something to do with the Imbolic festival when spring appears and the arrival of the sun defeats evil spirits, the pancake representing the sun.

Variations of pancakes, or **krampoth** in Cornish, are enjoyed all over the world in various guises: drop scones in Scotland, griddle cakes in parts of the US, crêpes in France, galettes in Brittany, pikelets in Australia and New Zealand and blini in Eastern Europe. Many customs, beliefs and traditions have evolved around them such as the 'pancake race'. The first recorded pancake race took place in 1445 in Olney, Buckinghamshire, the finish line of the race being at the church door. Pancake racing was recorded during the War of the Roses (1445 to 1487) and has continued through the centuries. The womenfolk of Olney in Buckinghamshire still fiercely uphold the tradition.

In Cornwall, we have Nickanan Night (sometimes called Hall Monday, Peasen Monday or Roguery Night), which is celebrated on the night before Shrove Tuesday, when it's OK to play practical jokes on family, friends and neighbours. The name Nickanan probably refers to knocking on doors and running away.

My friend Nicki Eathorne (born and raised in Four Lanes near Redruth) used to talk about her antics on Nickanan Night and recited this rhyme:

Nicka-nicka-nan
Give me some pancake
And then I'll be gone
But if you give me none
I'll throw a great stone
And down your door shall come

It's not exactly Shakespeare (who incidentally mentions pancakes in his plays) but it's an important part of our culture, one we should remember and record. Talking of which, the highest recorded pancake toss is 9.47m, flipping heck, that's high. I'm off to buy oranges, eggs and a step ladder!

Krampoth | Pancakes

Padel fria | Frying pan

Ple'ma ow fadel fria?
Where's my frying pan?

Yw hemma dha badel fria?
Is this your frying pan?

Yw. Hemm yw ow fadel fria
It is. That is my frying pan

Meur ras
Thank you

Gort kosel ha dybri krampoth
Keep calm and eat pancakes

Oy | Egg

Bleus | Flour

Leth | Milk

My a vynnsa kavos pymp krampoth, mar pleg
I would like five pancakes, please

My a vynn kavos ow krampoth gans sugen owraval ha sugra
I like to have my pancakes with orange and sugar

Ro dhymm krampoth, lemmyn, lemmyn lemmyn
Give me a pancake, now, now, now

Gone with the wind

It's a Saturday morning and I'm sat in *Receiver Coffee* – a very cool independent coffee shop in Charlottetown, Prince Edward Island, Canada. I'm waiting to meet Barb Morgan, a resident of the island whose family has Cornish roots.

Prince Edward Island (PEI) is Canada's smallest province and one of the many places Cornish migrants headed for in the 1800s, along with neighbouring maritime provinces New Brunswick and Nova Scotia.

PEI is also the birthplace of *Anne of Green Gables*, the novel written by Lucy Maud Montgomery in 1908, about Anne Shirley, an orphaned eleven-year-old girl who is adopted by a middle-aged brother and sister in the fictional town of Avonlea. *Anne of Green Gables* has been translated into twenty different languages, has sold more than fifty million copies worldwide and along with potatoes and lobster, is one of PEI's most precious commodities. You get a sense of Anne Shirley's wholesome lifestyle as you wander around this picturesque coastal town. Beautifully manicured, it feels partly (but very happily) stuck in 1908. The shiplap-clad, pastel coloured colonial houses and wide, tree-lined avenues add to the timeless charm of Charlottetown. I can imagine swishing my way along Great George Street dressed like Scarlett O'Hara in *Gone with the Wind*.

Barb arrives, introduces herself and quickly drags me back into the real world. I'm curious to find out about her Cornish origins.

What's your link to Cornwall, Barb?

"My great-grandfather James White, owned The White Swan in Fore Street, Looe at some point in the late1800s. His great-grandfather William White was a naval draughtsman. He was born in East Looe in 1790 and studied in Plymouth. William married Clarinda Triggs in 1812, they had a son who was baptised at Saint Martin's Church in Looe on 16th February 1817 – but by 1818 they were living here in Charlottetown, where he became a prominent shipbuilder. At that time, he was the only draughtsman on the island. He died in 1858 at York Point, PEI. William's sons, Clement and William Jr. also became shipbuilders in Charlottetown. There are lots of people of Cornish origin here, in fact there's even a town called Cornwall on the Island."

Later, Barb suggests we go for lunch. We take a short walk to Water Prince Corner Shop and Lobster Pound, which looks for all the world like a regular diner until you spot *the tank.* After a conversation-packed lunch of mussels, lobster and fries, Barb pulls out a black and white photograph of her great-grandfather, James White. He's incredibly handsome and I can easily imagine him being the landlord of a pub in Looe.

Prince Edward Island has beautiful beaches and is home to one of Canada's most impressive sea stacks – Teapot Rock. It's nearly time for me to leave though, so I'll have to visit Teapot Rock another time. The next stop on my Canadian adventure is Calgary, Alberta and the last time I was there it was 25 degrees below zero and deep in snow. Wish me luck.

Chons da! | Good luck!

Fatel yw an gewer yn Kanada?
How is the weather in Canada?

Hi a wra ergh | It's snowing

Fatel yw an gewer yn Kernow?
How is the weather in Cornwall?

Euthyk yw
It's awful

Hi a wra glaw
It is raining

Glyb yw | It's wet

Ha Gwynsek yw
And it's windy

Yma glaw pup dydh, dell hevel
There is rain every day, it seems

Ple'ma an howl? | Where is the sun?

An dhargan a leveris y fydh glyb ha gwynsek
The forecast says it will be wet and windy

Yma taran ha lughes haneth
There is this thunder and lightning tonight

Gyllys gans an gwyns
Gone with the wind

Going up Camborne Hill

On the corner of Cross Street and Trevenson Street in Camborne, stands a monument to Richard Trevithick; a sculpture by LS Merrifield which was completed in 1928. The gilded bronze statue shows Trevithick holding a model of a steam locomotive and a set of callipers. He stands aloft a plinth displaying four ornate plaques depicting a sail ship, a Cornish boiler, a Merthyr Tydfil Locomotive and an iron steam and sail ship.

Richard Trevithick was born in Illogan in 1771. He invented high-pressure steam engines which were used in local and international mines. The son of a mine captain and miner's daughter, Richard Trevithick was a prolific inventor who built what is widely considered to be the first automobile. He nicknamed his creation the *Puffing Devil* and successfully tested it by going up Camborne Hill on Christmas Eve 1801, a journey that provided the inspiration for the well-known Cornish folk song *'Camborne Hill'*. Among numerous other things, Richard Trevithick also invented 'Cornish Boilers', which were installed in the existing pumping engines at Dolcoath Mine, more than doubling their efficiency.

Trevithick spent over a decade exploring the mining potential of Peru and Costa Rica before dying, penniless, in 1833.

Trevithick Day, established 150 years after Richard Trevithick's death in 1983 is a community event that takes place on the last Saturday of April each year. It has quickly become an important part of the Cornish calendar. Attracting thousands of visitors, the free one-day festival see's Camborne's streets filled with bal maidens and steam engines in a celebration of Camborne's links with Trevithick and local mining heritage. Let's hope the April showers stay away on Trevithick Day.

LS Merrifield was an interesting sculptor who worked from the end of the 19th Century through to the end of WW2. Specialising in portrait sculpture, Merrifield designed several WW1 memorials featuring figures, including the soldier monument outside the former Duke of Cornwall's Light Infantry garrison in Bodmin – now Cornwall's Regimental Museum. Merrifield trained at Cheltenham School of Art and the Royal Academy School in 1904. He became a Fellow of the Royal Society of British Sculpture in 1926, and he completed his sculpture of Richard Trevithick at the height of his career.

It's amazing how many public sculptures and monuments there are here in Kernow. I particularly appreciate the statues of Richard Trevithick in Camborne, Anne Glanville and Isambard Kingdom Brunel in Saltash, Humphry Davy in Penzance, the Tin Miner in Redruth, The Drummer and Richard Lander in Truro, the fisherman in Newlyn – all beautiful, visual reminders of our industrial heritage and the foundations of our community. The change-makers; the social influencers of their time.

Gav dhymm, mes henn yw ow delow, dell dybav
Excuse me, but I think that's my statue

Kowas Ebrel
April showers

Glaw, glaw ha moy glaw
Rain, rain and more rain

Mir orth henna! Jynn-ethen!
Look at that! A steam engine!

Ple'ma an ogassa bre?
Where is the nearest hill?

Yn Kambronn | In Camborne

Nyns yw unn jynn-ethen nevra lowr
One steam-engine is never enough

Genys o yn Illogan | I was born in Illogan

A pyth eur yw? | What time is it?

Eth eur | Eight o'clock

Cornish by Design

Did you know that Cornwall Council has been campaigning for a Cornish tick box option to be included in the ethnic origin section of the Census since 1992?

Speaking about a 2018 creative project involving a double-decker bus and a Cornish citizenship quiz MP George Eustace recently said, *"I am working with my Cornish colleagues to campaign for a Cornish tick box on the census, and I am hopeful that this will go ahead. Many people locally identify themselves as 'Cornish' and there has been a considerable revival of interest in Cornish culture and language of late."*

Gemma Goodman, Project Manager explained, *"Each person entered the bus through mock security with passport officers (lovely volunteers) operating the security scanner. They then answered a few questions from a Cornish citizenship quiz. It was a safe and friendly space where people could discuss Cornishness, what it means to them, and their own identity. We saw an overwhelmingly positive response to the question 'Would you support the inclusion of a Cornish tick box* at the next Census' *with 96% of responses saying yes. This included both people who do and who do not themselves identify as Cornish."*

The thought-provoking project captured the imagination of people in Cornwall, Devon and Somerset. One thousand six hundred members of the public supported Cornish distinctiveness, identifying themselves as Cornish by birth, by ancestry, by marriage, by design or by accident.

Hundreds of thousands of people worldwide are Cornish by descent. Many of them celebrate their ancestry, roots and homeland even if they've never set foot on Cornish soil. It's part of their identity.

Our roots are our anchor, one constant in an ever-changing world. Our circumstances can alter daily, things begin and end, people come and go, the world turns and seasons change. Painful endings bring unexpected opportunities as well as exciting beginnings. Through the trials and tribulations of life our roots are a grounding influence, they give us a sense of belonging. Where do you come from? Do you identify yourself as Cornish? Perhaps, like me, you have a strong affinity with Cornwall but can't explain why. I have Breton ancestry and feel a strong connection with all the Celtic nations.

I've lived in Cornwall longer than I've lived anywhere else and feel at home here.

I certainly feel a sense of homesickness when I'm away from Cornwall, as if I'm slightly displaced. There's a Cornish word to describe that intangible sense of longing, it's *hireth*.

If there was a census tick box for Cornish at heart, I'd tick it. In the meantime, I'm Cornish by design.

A bleth os ta devedhys?
Where do you come from?

Hedh an kyttrin na!
Hold that bus!

Py kyttrin rag Resrudh, mar pleg?
Which bus for Redruth, please?

A wra an kyttrin ma hedhi yn Hellys?
Does this bus stop at Helston?

Dhe by eur a dhiberth an kyttrin?
What time does the bus leave?

Eth eur | Eight o'clock

An kyttrin yw ugens mynysenn yn diwedhes
The bus is twenty minutes late

Eus esedhow gesys? | Are there any seats left?

Gav dhymm, mes henn yw ow hador, dell dybav
Excuse me, but I think that's my seat

My a vynn mos tre lemmyn …
I want to go home now …

Thanks

— Kirstie Newton, the formidable editor of the award-winning international lifestyle and culture magazine *Cornwall Today* for giving me the opportunity to fulfil a life-long ambition of writing a regular column.

— Mark Trevethan, my Cornish language teacher, and my original Cornish language classmates Chloe Phillips, Tamsin Daniel, Vicky Reece-Romain and Edward Rowe for many cheese-related laughs.

— Ken George, who has translated my song lyrics into Cornish since 2014, for his support and brilliance.

— Andrew Morris, for sharing his passion for and knowledge of traditional Cornish culture.

— Sam Kelly, Jamie Francis, Evan Carson, Morrigan Palmer Brown, Alan Pengelly, Mark Barnwell, Annie Baylis, Caz Davey, Gareth Lee and Ryan Jones for many wonderful adventures in Cornish music.

— Andrew Jones and Carys Barriball for endless laughs and straight-talking advice.

— Elina Kansikas and Stephen Tolfrey for creating beautiful images and film for my various Cornish projects.

— Ken and Sue Terry and Norma and Alan Dobinson of Looe Old Cornwall Society, for their tireless work promoting Cornishness in the South East Cornwall area.

Special thanks

— Gareth Rhys Jones, for his love and encouragement.

— P&M, for giving me the space to by myself, as well as their mother.

— My mum, Dorothy, for being the only person in the family who bothers to read my articles.

— Maggie Greenwood and Nicki Eathorne, my soul mates in song.

— Finally, thanks to all the people who have told me 'no' in life. You know who you are. You have been a constant source of motivation.

About the author

Tanya Brittain describes herself as a cultural ambassador, Cornish language student, writer and tea drinker. Tanya has Breton ancestry but was born and raised in South Yorkshire, England. She graduated from Art college in the 80s and her first job was in the mining industry as an illustrator of specialist equipment for technical publications. She progressed rapidly through the ranks into general management and marketing. Working in the publishing, food and music industries over a period of twenty years, she ended up in Cornwall working on a six-month project. Six months became six years, six years became twelve, etc.

Working actively with other Celtic nations and connecting with Cornish diaspora worldwide, Tanya has made an outstanding contribution to the promotion of Cornwall's traditional culture, heritage and language over the past decade.

An award-winning writer, songwriter and touring musician, Tanya formed folk band, **The Changing Room**, with vocalist Sam Kelly in 2014. Her original music in Cornish language has been broadcast live on BBC Radio 4, BBC Radio 3 and BBC Radio 2 and recordings by The Changing Room are afforded regular airplay worldwide. The Changing Room's debut album is listed in *The Telegraph's* 'Best Folk albums of 2015'. Tanya has commissioned and produced many live performances, short films and vox pops featuring famous faces speaking or singing in Cornish. The Artistic Director of a large music festival for over five years, Tanya was responsible for designing and delivering several projects involving the creation of new music in both English and Cornish language, including the Big Cornish Sing – a live broadcast which attracted a digital reach of almost two million viewers.

Tanya has been writing a monthly bi-lingual column for international cultural lifestyle magazine *Cornwall Today* for over two years and has now turned her attention to writing full-time.